FREE TO A GOOD HOME

Colin Thompson

RANDOM HOUSE AUSTRALIA

They collected strange and unusual things, because Mr Smith always said you could never tell when something might come in handy.

Other children collected stray animals - maybe a lost dog or an unwanted cat, which wasn't always lost or unwanted, just mislaid.

But the Smith children, Peter and Sally, collected an old lady.

They found her at the shopping mall and took her home with them.

'It's okay, Mum,' said Sally. 'You're always telling us you could do with an extra pair of hands around the place.'

The old lady sat at the kitchen table drinking a cup of tea with a nice little old lady smile on her face.

'But she must belong somewhere,' said Mrs Smith.

'No I don't,' said the little old lady.

'There'll be people looking for her,' said Mr Smith.

'No there won't,' said the little old lady.

She dunked another biscuit in her tea and did some more smiling.

There were five people in the room and three of them looked very happy. Only Mr and Mrs Smith looked worried, and they were not so much worried as confused.

'You can't just go around collecting old people,' said Mrs Smith.

'Why not?' Sally asked.

'Well, she's old,' said Mrs Smith as nicely as she could, 'and old people forget things like where they live. There's probably a family getting really worried about her.'

'No there isn't,' said the old lady.

Things got no better when Mr Smith phoned the police. They said that if anyone had lost an old lady, they hadn't told them about it, but of course that sort of thing did happen and people who had lost an old person were often too ashamed to call the police.

The old lady cleared the tea things off the table and washed them up. Then she made another pot of tea and baked the most wonderful cake the Smiths had ever tasted.

'What's your name, dear?' said Mrs Smith as she ate her third slice of cake.

'You know,' said the old lady, 'I've never liked the one I grew up with. I think I'll have a new one. My new name will be Granny.'

'Yes, but what's your proper name, dear?' said Mr Smith.

'Granny,' said the old lady. 'And you don't need to keep calling me dear, dear. I'm not senile or stupid.'

'Granny's a great name,' said Peter.

'And you can be our granny, because we've never had one of them,' said Sally.

'Well that's settled then,' said the old lady, 'because I've never had any grandchildren either.'

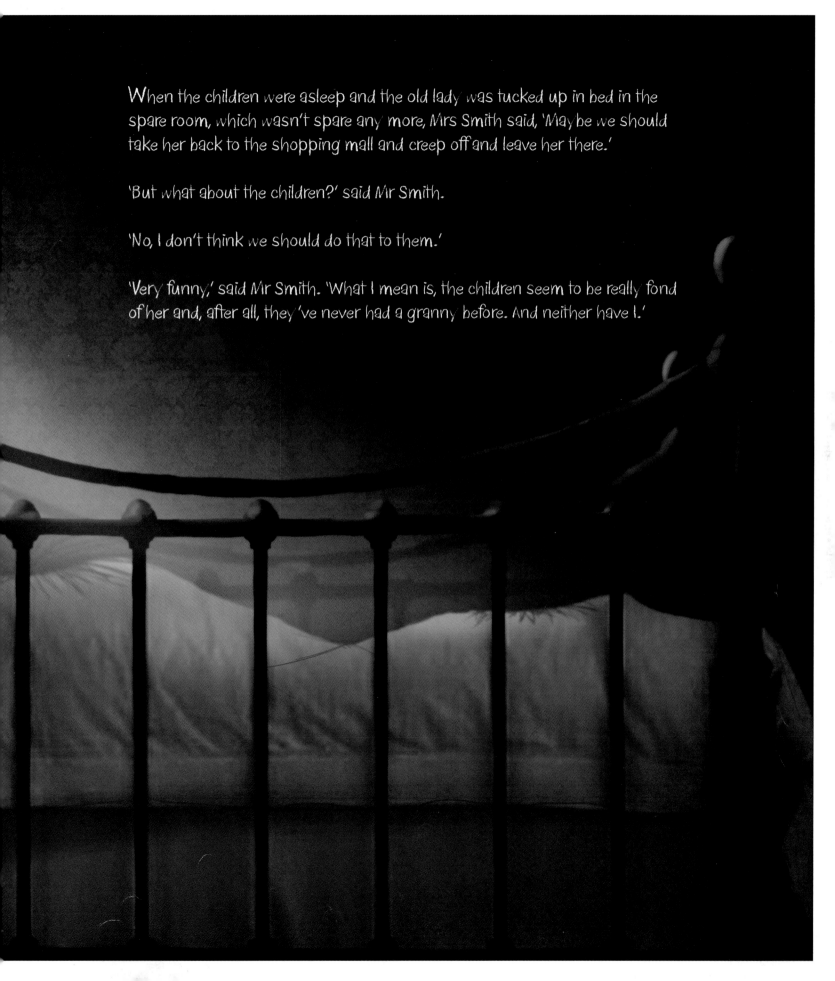

When the children were asleep and the old lady was tucked up in bed in the spare room, which wasn't spare any more, Mrs Smith said, 'Maybe we should take her back to the shopping mall and creep off and leave her there.'

'But what about the children?' said Mr Smith.

'No, I don't think we should do that to them.'

'Very funny,' said Mr Smith. 'What I mean is, the children seem to be really fond of her and, after all, they've never had a granny before. And neither have I.'

Mr Smith's parents had fallen down a very deep hole
when he was only five years old. They had been out
looking for their parents who had also fallen down the
same very deep hole. This meant that although Mr
Smith's parents had found his grandparents, Mr Smith
had grown up as an orphan.

This was one reason he was quite happy to have the old lady move in with them.

Mrs Smith should have been equally happy, because she was an orphan too, but just collecting an old lady like you might collect your dry cleaning took a bit of getting used to.

Mrs Smith's parents and grandparents had not fallen down a very deep hole. That would have been an unbelievable coincidence. No, they had been abducted by aliens and were now living as exhibits in a zoo on a planet many light years from Earth.

The old lady brought Mr and Mrs Smith tea in bed the next morning. She gave the children breakfast and got them off to school while Mrs Smith relaxed in a warm bath with extra lavender oil.

Later, Mrs Smith said, 'Now I'm worried about something else.'

'You like worrying about things,' said Mr Smith. 'It gives you a huge sense of achievement when you find a way to stop worrying about them.'

'No I don't,' said Mrs Smith. 'But supposing we let her stay and we all get really fond of her and then someone comes along and takes her away?'

'I don't think she'd want to go,' said Mr Smith, looking out the window to where the old lady was sitting in the middle of the grass sharpening the blades on the lawnmower. 'She looks as if she's never been so happy in all her life.'

And she hadn't.

When the children came home from school, Granny showed Mr Smith how to make a fantastic steak and kidney pie. She showed Peter how to do his nineteen-and-a-half times table and taught Sally all the tenses of the verb 'borrow' in French and Spanish. Then she put up the kitchen shelves that had been waiting in their box for so long that three generations of mice had been born there.

$$19\frac{1}{2} \times 1 = 18\frac{1}{2}+$$

$$19\frac{1}{2} \times 2 = 39$$

$$19\frac{1}{2} \times 3 = 58.5$$

$$19\frac{1}{2} \times 4 = 78$$

$$19\frac{1}{2} \times 7 = 136.5$$

$$19\frac{1}{2} \times 8 = \text{TUESDAY} \quad \text{SUNDAY}$$

$$19\frac{1}{2} \times 5 = 97.5$$

$$19\frac{1}{2} \times 6 = 117$$

$$\frac{1}{2} \times 19\frac{1}{2} = \text{LOTS}$$

$$19\frac{1}{2} \times 0 = 3.30$$

None of these were the sort of thing Mr and Mrs Smith were any good at. Mrs Smith's cooking only ever had one flavour - burnt. Mr Smith's handyman efforts always needed several sticking plasters followed by a phone call to a professional handyman who ended up charging them twice as much as if they had got him to do the job in the first place. And homework was a foreign country that Mr and Mrs Smith had never visited.

It became very obvious very quickly, though no one ever said it out loud, that the one thing their lives had lacked all these years was an old lady.

THE MIGHTY
WALLACE

Now they had one and their family was complete.

'Except for a Grandad,' said Sally, but everyone pretended they hadn't heard her.

See, you *can* choose your relatives

A Random House book
Published by Random House Australia Pty Ltd
Level 3, 100 Pacific Highway, North Sydney NSW 2060
www.randomhouse.com.au

First published by Random House Australia in 2009

Addresses for companies within the Random House Group can be found at www.randomhouse.com.au/offices.

National Library of Australia
Cataloguing-in-Publication Entry

Thompson, Colin (Colin Edward)

Free to a good home / Colin Thompson

ISBN 978 1 74166 318 1 (hbk.)
ISBN 978 1 74166 319 8 (pbk.)

A823.4

Cover and text design by Colin Thompson
Printed and bound in China by C&C Offset Printing Co., Ltd

10 9 8 7 6 5 4 3 2 1

Visit Colin Thompson's website: http://www.colinthompson.com

The bathtub is based on a painting by Monet, except he was too shortsighted to see the submarine.

PLEASE NOTE: Incredible amounts of chocolate cake were harmed during the making of this book.

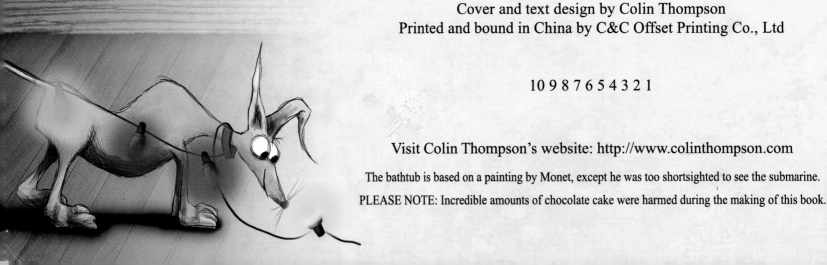